THE SUMMER DOLPHIN

*For the amazing campaigners working
to protect dolphins around the world.*
HW

In memoriam Alan Dean 1946–2023
DD

LITTLE TIGER
An imprint of Little Tiger Press Limited
1 Coda Studios, 189 Munster Road,
London SW6 6AW

Imported into the EEA by Penguin Random House Ireland,
Morrison Chambers, 32 Nassau Street, Dublin D02 YH68

www.littletiger.co.uk

A paperback original
First published in Great Britain in 2024

Text copyright © Holly Webb, 2024
Illustrations copyright © David Dean, 2024
Author photograph copyright © Lou Abercrombie

ISBN: 978-1-78895-706-9

A CIP catalogue record for this book is available
from the British Library.

Printed and bound in the UK.

The Forest Stewardship Council® (FSC®) is a global, not-for-profit organization
dedicated to the promotion of responsible forest management worldwide. FSC®
defines standards based on agreed principles for responsible forest stewardship
that are supported by environmental, social, and economic stakeholders.
To learn more, visit www.fsc.org

2 4 6 8 10 9 7 5 3 1

"But which is my bed?" Lillie asked, looking around the tiny room. It was just – only just – big enough for two single beds, with a narrow strip of floor between them. Her sister Frankie had raced up the stairs before her, and flung her bag on one of the beds, and the other was already covered in a scatter of her cousin Lara's things.

"There isn't one," Lara said, smirking. "You can't sleep in here with us, you're too little."

"But Gran said we were all together…" Lillie poked at the sliding doors in the wall, in case they magically turned into a space for another bed, but they only hid what was obviously a wardrobe.

"You can sleep in the cupboard if you like," Lara giggled.

"Don't be mean, Lara." Lara's mum, Lillie and Frankie's auntie Sasha, appeared in the doorway. "I'm sorry, Lillie, you've got the short straw. There aren't enough bedrooms for all of us, when the whole family's here, so you're sharing with Frankie and Lara, but one of you has to have a sleeping bag and a blow-up mattress down the middle there."

Lillie stared at the strip of floor between the beds. She knew exactly what would happen. Lara and Frankie would spend the whole fortnight of their holiday accidentally on purpose stomping on her as they got in and out of bed. And somehow it would always be her fault for getting in their way.

Why hadn't she beaten Frankie to the top of the stairs?

"Can't we take it in turns to have the sleeping bag?" she asked, and Auntie Sasha nodded.

"That's a really good idea."

Lillie could tell from the icy burn on the back of her neck that both her big sister and her cousin were giving her a glare. She had a feeling that her chances of getting them to swap their comfy beds for the sleeping bag and blow-up mattress that Auntie Sasha was pulling out of the cupboard were slim.

She sighed and followed Auntie Sasha back downstairs to fetch her bag. She'd been looking forward to this holiday for ages – the last two weeks of the summer break before they went

back to school. Her gran and grandpa had just
retired and moved house from Swansea to the
Gower – a rocky finger of land pointing out into
the sea. Lillie and Frankie and her mum and
dad had been on holiday to the Gower before,
but always camping, or in a hired cottage.
Now Lillie's family – and two sets of aunts
and uncles and cousins – were staying in their
grandparents' new house, all at the same time.

Mum said she thought Gran and Grandpa
were "gluttons for punishment, but if that's the
way they want to do it…" Then she'd trailed off
into a meaningful silence.

"They've only just finished redecorating and
putting the new bathrooms in," Dad pointed
out. "The house wasn't ready earlier, that's why
they're having everyone now."

"Rather them than me," Mum muttered,

but even she was excited about the holiday. The weather forecast was looking good and Lillie couldn't wait to go from a big city to the seaside. Gran had sent them the most amazing photos of the new house, and the beach it was close to. There were loads of walks and cliffs and climbs to explore too, she'd promised.

"It's going to be a full house," she'd told Lillie on the phone, only the day before. "I'm really looking forward to having you all to stay – I'm hoping we can do it every summer! You'll help me with the food, won't you, Lillie? I know how much you like cooking, and this house has a beautiful big kitchen."

"Yes!" Lillie had beamed into the phone. Gran always let her cook much more exciting things than Mum and Dad did, and Lillie had worried that the new house and all the family staying

would change that somehow. Gran's little
kitchen, with the tiny square table heaped up
with cake tins and the overflowing box of biscuit
cutters and cake decorations, had been one
of Lillie's favourite ever places. There was still
an aching space in her middle when she thought
of it belonging to someone else.

Maybe even someone who didn't like to cook.

"All my cooking stuff's come with us, Lillie,"
Gran had reminded her gently. "There's just
a bit more room for it all now. Your grandpa
says I'm not allowed to buy anything else to
fill up the space…"

"But we could buy them for you!" Lillie
pointed out. "Christmas presents!"

"That's true, we could get around him that
way! I've always wanted a pasta machine, so
maybe I'll put it on my Christmas list."

Right now Lillie didn't feel much like Gran's special kitchen helper. She felt like an afterthought who'd been squashed in between the two older girls.

"Did you find where you're sleeping?" Gran said, coming to give her a hug. "I didn't catch you before you raced upstairs!" she added, squeezing Lillie tight. "I'm sorry the three of you are in that little attic room. You, Frankie and Lara were meant to have the bigger room down here, but Leon's managed to twist his ankle! He can't go up and down the stairs easily, so we had to swap everyone around, so he and Charlie were on the ground floor. It wasn't planned that way."

"Oh…" Lillie nodded. That wasn't so bad then. Gran and Grandpa hadn't meant for them all to be squished. "It's fine," she said, perking up. "I'll fit, Gran, don't worry."

"I've saved whipping up the cream for the pavlovas for you," Gran told her. "I know you love using the mixer."

"Did you get pineapple?" Lillie asked, eyeing her suspiciously.

"Of course I got pineapple!" Gran swooped in to hug her again. "Oh, I have missed you. Mind you, how any grandchild of mine thinks pineapple should go on a pavlova, I don't know…"

Spending time with Gran was one of the things that Lillie had been really looking forward to about this holiday. But she hadn't thought she would be left with Gran or her parents *all the time*. Usually she and Frankie got on really well, and they hardly ever argued – or not really, anyway. Just moaning about who had eaten the last of the good cereal, or who got to go in the front seat of the car, that kind of thing. On this holiday everything had shifted. Suddenly Frankie and Lara were the big, grown-up cousins, and Lillie was the little one. The one who got left out all the time because the older girls had their own plans.

It seemed to happen without Lillie having any say at all. It had started with the bedroom – with Frankie and Lara making it up the stairs before her, and somehow turning themselves into a gang of two that had no room for anyone else. When everyone – even Leon, hopping

impressively fast on his crutches – headed down
to the beach with a picnic that Gran must have
spent all morning putting together, Lara and
Frankie sped on ahead down the path. They set
up camp next to a couple of big rocks, and it
looked like it was just for them. Lillie didn't think
she was allowed to go and sit on that flowery rug,
even if Frankie was her sister. The two older girls
were radiating go-away vibes. Lillie looked at
them for a moment and then went to help
Gran unpack the cool boxes.

Frankie sat next to her while they were eating lunch, and even shared the last chocolate-chip cookie with her, and Lillie wondered if she'd been imagining the weird go-away force field from earlier on. But when Gran finally announced that it was long enough after lunch for people to go in the sea, Frankie and Lara disappeared down the beach before Lillie had even got her swimming costume on.

They were messing around with one of the foam bodyboards, pushing each other on and off, and Lillie was desperate to join them. She got her swimsuit on at last and padded over the pale sand to where the tiny waves were hitting the beach. The sea was so calm, the waves were hardly there, and they came up on to the sand with nothing more than a low swoosh. The water even looked warm –

it was a soft greenish, brownish sort of blue.
But it was actually quite cold, Lillie found,
when she dipped her toes in.

Her sister and cousin were only a few metres
in – Gran had warned them that there was
quite a steep shelf on this bay, they'd be out
of their depth quickly if they went too far
out – and Lillie knew that they'd seen her.
Lara glanced right through her, as though she
wasn't there, but Lillie saw Frankie notice her
watching. Her sister paused for a moment,
standing in the water and looking at Lillie
over Lara's shoulder. There was an uncertain,
worried expression on her face. But then it
smoothed away and she squealed and splashed
Lara, and became wilder and brighter and even
more grown-up and part of a pair who didn't
want anyone else.

Lillie sat down at the edge of the water and stuck her feet in the sea, feeling the wavelets suck the sand back around her toes.

What was going on? Frankie had never abandoned her like this before. Even when she'd gone up to secondary school, she still let Lillie walk with her and a couple of friends, if she didn't mind leaving early. Sometimes Frankie let Lillie borrow her phone to watch YouTube videos, and she loved planning movie nights for them both and Mum, with popcorn and everyone wearing onesies. Lillie had always thought that Frankie was the very best sort of big sister. Now Lara had stolen her away.

It wasn't as if they'd never met Lara before, Lillie thought, piling up a tiny cairn of stones. They saw her and Auntie Sasha every so often – just not all the time, as they lived quite far

away. Lara was about six months older than
Frankie and in the school year above, but
she'd never acted like this to Lillie before,
they'd always messed around together.
Now it was as if all those sleepovers and
trips had never happened. This Lara seemed
years and years older.

"You OK, petal?" Dad had crept
up behind Lillie without
her noticing, and she
jumped. She'd been
concentrating hard
on the pebbles, so it
didn't look like she was
watching Lara and
Frankie. Watching
them and wanting
to be with them.

She was trying very, very hard to show she didn't care in the slightest.

It was possibly not working very well.

"I'm fine," she said grumpily, pushing the little tower of stones over.

"You want to go in the sea with me? Is it freezing? I blew up the turtle…"

Lillie looked up and realized that her dad was carrying the huge, inflatable turtle that she and Lara had begged for last summer when they went on their first holiday abroad, to Spain. Everyone on the beach had some sort of boat or raft or fantastic animal, it seemed, and they'd fallen in love with the turtle's sweet grin. He was big enough for one of them to sit on, or both if they didn't mind falling off again quite quickly, which was all part of the fun.

Lillie's dad plunged into the sea, muttering,

"Oh wow, oh wow, that's cold," and then, "Uuurrrgggghhh," and then, "It's actually quite nice when you're in," in an encouraging way to Lillie. He launched the turtle further, spreadeagled himself on top of it, and slowly slid off backwards.

Lillie giggled and tiptoed into the sea after him. She knew it was better to rush in all at once and get it over with, but she still couldn't quite bring herself to do it. She had to go bit by bit. Eventually she caught up with Dad, and ducked the back of her head under the water – shivering happily as she felt that strange buzzing down the back of her neck that meant she was properly in the sea. Then she wriggled up on top of the turtle, gripping the handles tight, and basked in the bright sun reflecting off the water.

"Dad! Dad! Can we have a go?"

Lillie's eyes snapped open as a wash of freezing water slapped over her back. Frankie or Lara – she wasn't sure which – had just splashed her. Worse – they wanted the turtle.

"But I'm on it!" Lillie protested.

"You can all share it," Dad said, entirely failing to notice that anything was going on. He'd seen Frankie and Lara ignoring her earlier on, Lillie thought. How could he think everything was OK and they were all going to mess around in the sea together? "I'll watch you from the beach, OK? Don't go any further out. I reckon you're probably just on the edge of your depth here."

"Uh-huh." Lara nodded briskly and flung herself on top of the turtle, grabbing one of the handles. "Move over, Lillie! Don't hog it!"

"I'm not…" Lillie spluttered as she slid backwards over the turtle's flipper and into the water. She watched indignantly as Lara and Frankie bounced and splashed – and somehow, whenever she reached for one of the handles, or tried to climb on to the turtle's tail, one of the older ones would somehow be in the way and she'd slide back into the water.

"Nice time?" Mum asked brightly as Lillie trailed back up the beach.

Lillie just stared at her. She supposed that from the beach it might actually have looked as if they were all playing together. If you entirely failed to notice that Lillie had spent the whole time falling into the water.

"You'll get cold, sweetheart, put your poncho on." Mum handed Lillie her stripey robe and went back to chatting with Auntie Sasha.

Couldn't she make up her own mind whether she was cold? Why did Mum have to treat her like a baby? Maybe that was why Lara and Frankie were doing it too… Lillie wriggled into the poncho – which was actually very cosy – and sat down gloomily on the edge of the rug.

Dad was still keeping an eye on Frankie and Lara, and the rest of the adults were talking. Leon and Charlie were playing a weird cross between cricket and tennis with a Frisbee and Leon's crutches. It didn't look as if it was a game that three people could play.

What if the whole of the holiday was like this?

"Mmmph! What are you doing?" Lillie
blinked up grumpily from her cosy nest of
sleeping bag and blankets. "You're standing
on me! Get off!"

"I can't!" Lara snapped back. "You're in the
way. I'm going to the loo. Why do you have
to lie just *there*? You're obviously going to get
trodden on!"

Lillie wriggled furiously, trying to get
Lara off her arm – it was hurting. Lara yelped.
"Hey! I nearly fell over! Watch it!"

"You – were – standing – on – me!" Lillie

snarled back. "Where else am I going to lie? This is where my bed is! You watch where you're putting your big feet!"

"Be quiet, Lillie! I'm trying to sleep," Frankie growled from the other bed.

At this point, Lara kicked Lillie – Lillie wasn't sure if it was on purpose or not as they were all in the dark and it was quite hard to tell what was Lillie and what was floor, but she was fairly sure Lara had meant to be mean. Lillie surged up off the floor, like some sort of sleeping-bag caterpillar, and (definitely on purpose, but if anyone asked she was going to claim it was an accident) elbowed her cousin in the stomach. Then she waddled out of the room surprisingly fast for someone still wrapped in a sleeping bag and two blankets, but she was very cross.

Lillie sat on the first step of the attic stairs so she could bump her way down. Trying to walk in a sleeping bag seemed dangerous, and she was still half asleep and cosy, and she didn't think of unzipping it and getting out. She could hear a muttered  conversation going on between Frankie and Lillie as she squirmed down the stairs.

"Where's she going?" That was her cousin.

"I don't know! Did you tread on her?"

"A little bit? It's not like I meant to – she was in the way!"

"Nnnngh, she'll get us in trouble, Lara."

"It wasn't *my* fault." Lara, sounding a mix of self-righteous and worried. "It's just like your stupid little sister to go and tell."

Lillie felt a flash of angry heat wash up around her ears, and knew she'd gone scarlet. She wasn't planning to tell anyone, she just wanted somewhere to sleep where people weren't going to stomp on her! Until now she'd been a bit fed up with Lara and her sister. Now she was definitely *angry*.

She got to the bottom of the stairs and shuffle-stomped across the landing to the window. It had a seat in front, she'd noticed it earlier today while she was carrying her bag up. It was padded too, with a long, narrow cushion. Lillie hadn't thought of it as a comfy bed when she went past it before, but now it came without

snarky older cousins and horrible big sisters
trying to trample on her and then blame her
for it, and it looked wonderful. Lillie wriggled
herself on to the window seat and sighed crossly.
They could have their stupid room. It wasn't as if
she wanted to be anywhere near them.

She turned over, hunching the sleeping
bag up around her shoulders, and fell asleep,
still furious.

"I've got a treat arranged for us today."
Grandpa beamed at everyone around the
breakfast table. "I've booked us a boat."

Everyone stared back at him. "A boat to
where?" Mum asked, sounding a little worried.

"Oh, don't worry, love, you won't need your
passports. Just a trip around the bay, but the

people who run it are experts at finding seals and dolphins. It's a wildlife-watching trip."

"Dolphins?" Lillie's voice came out in a squeak. She'd never imagined there would be wild dolphins close to Gran and Grandpa's house. They felt like such a magical, deep-sea thing. She could see Frankie doing a superior raised-eyebrows face to Lara about the squeaking but she didn't care. It *was* special. "Will we really see them?"

"Well, I can't promise," Grandpa admitted. "But they said it was very likely. Apparently there's a pod of dolphins that have been seen up and down the coast this summer."

"Cool! Do they come close to the boat?" Leon asked.

Grandpa nodded. "They're very nosy, the man from the boat company told me.

They like to investigate what's going on in their water."

"I'd love to see a seal as well," Mum put in. "I've always liked them, such sweet faces. Thanks, Dad. What a nice thing to plan for us."

"We've got to get down to the beach by ten." Grandpa went back to munching toast, looking pleased with the success of his surprise. "Bring waterproofs, and you need to wear shoes that can get wet, like those ones you've got for going in the sea."

"How do we get in?" Mum hissed as they stood on the beach looking at the boat. "It's all the way out *there*, and we're *here*…"

"Ah…" Grandpa looked slightly guilty. "We have to wade out to it. But the water's not meant to be higher than knee-deep. I was supposed to tell everyone to wear shorts, as well as the shoes bit, I remember that now. Or trousers you can roll up." He looked hopefully at Mum's legs. "You can roll those up, Bella, can't you?"

Mum sighed and started trying to scrunch up her leggings.

"I have to say, this is a slightly smaller boat than I was expecting," Gran murmured, eyeing the orange and black inflatable bobbing on the water. "I hope it's not too wobbly."

"It looks great," Charlie said enthusiastically. "It's like a lifeboat. I bet it goes really fast. You booked the whole boat just for us, Grandpa? That's so cool."

"Brilliant," Leon agreed. His ankle was feeling recovered enough that he'd left his crutches back at the house.

The boat's captain, whose name was Pete, came over with a huge armful of life jackets. "You've picked a lovely day for it!" he called.

Grandpa nodded graciously, as though he'd personally arranged the sunshine.

Pete and his crewmate Alice went round doling out life jackets and showing everyone how to do up the straps. Lillie's was bulky – it felt hard to move her arms – but she didn't mind. She liked messing around in the shallows but she wasn't the world's best swimmer, and Gran and Charlie were right, the boat looked fast *and* wobbly. A life jacket felt like a very good idea.

Once everyone was kitted out, Alice led them into the water towards the boat, which was called the *Mermaid*. Lillie was glad she'd worn her favourite yellow shorts, as she was

pretty sure she wouldn't get them wet –
Mum had already stopped in the middle
of the sea to try and roll her leggings up
another few centimetres. The sea was warmer
than it had been the day before, she thought,
or maybe it was just because she was wearing
her waterproof anorak. Alice stood at the
side of the boat, helping everyone to heave
themselves in. The rows of seats made it feel
a bit like a bus – but surrounded by clear,
deep-blue water. Lillie leaned over the fat,
rounded side of the boat, peering into
the sea.

"Watch out, Lillie, not so far!" Mum's voice
had a slightly panicky note to it.

"I'm not! Honestly, Mum. I just wanted
to look at the water – I think I can see the
bottom, it's so clear!"

"Isn't it beautiful?" Alice said, smiling as she climbed in to sit in the row behind. "I'm hoping we'll see lots out there today. I'm your wildlife guide as well as crew. I'm here to help you spot everything."

"Dolphins?" Lillie asked eagerly.

"If we're lucky. We saw them on our trips yesterday and the day before – a pod of four, and they stayed with us for ages." Alice was beaming – Lillie could tell she was excited about the dolphins too, even though she must have seen them heaps of times. "I can't promise though," she warned.

Once everyone was on board and Pete had given them a quick safety briefing – basically, don't fall out – he started up the engine and they moved slowly out to sea, heading along the coast. Alice had binoculars and she was scanning around, looking for seabirds as well as seals and dolphins. She pointed out several different seabirds – a white fulmar that skimmed over the water just beside the boat for a few seconds, and a few black-and-white birds that Lillie thought might be penguins for a second, until Alice said they were guillemots.

"They nest at Worm's Head," she explained. "That's where we're heading. It's a tidal island – so it's joined to the mainland at low tide, and you can walk out to it, but at high tide the sea cuts it off. It's actually a wild bird reserve for most of the summer months, to protect the nests."

"I've read about that!" Mum put in. "I was hoping we could go for a walk out to it. It's not far from Gran and Grandpa's house, only a couple of miles. I think it's this weekend that it opens up again."

"You should definitely do that," Alice said, smiling. "Most of the birds will have left, but you'll see the seals, and maybe dolphins. They're often round there. And it's just

a really beautiful place. So wild-looking. You'll
see, the way the rocks make a bridge, it's really
dramatic. A little bit scary to walk over, though!"

Lillie was listening to Mum and Alice
chatting about the seabirds, and how special
the island was as a nesting site, but she was
leaning on the side of the boat and gazing into
the still water. There were hardly any waves and
the sea was a brilliant clear greeny blue. Every
so often the shadow of a tiny cloud settled over
them, and the water seemed to turn to ink.
Lillie was tired still, after Lara waking her the
night before, and the soft rocking of the boat
was making her sleepy. She was seeing things,
down in the water. A huge jellyfish was floating
towards them, its bell-shaped top pulsing in and
out. Lillie gazed at it dreamily, and then blinked
as a drop of water splashed her cheek.

She was sharply awake again – and the jellyfish was still there!

"Look!" she squeaked huskily, and then louder, "Alice, look! A jellyfish!"

"Oh, well spotted!" Alice said delightedly. "That's a barrel jellyfish. Pete, slow down!"

Pete eased to a gentle glide, sweeping round in a smooth curve so that everyone could get a glimpse of the jellyfish without having to lean over to the same side of the boat.

"It's enormous!" Leon gasped. "Does it sting? Is it poisonous?"

Charlie quickly stopped trying to dip his hand in the water.

"They do sting, but only really, really lightly," Alice explained. "Some people don't even feel them, and most people who do get stung say it only feels like a nettle sting. You're lucky to see such a huge one! Sometimes they get called dustbin-lid jellyfish, because they're usually the size of a dustbin lid, but this one's a lot bigger than that. Maybe eighty centimetres across? Look, you can see the purple frilly edge around the bell."

"I didn't know we could get jellyfish that big in the sea around here," Grandpa said, shaking his head. "It will make me think twice about swimming."

Alice grinned at him. "I promise they're usually smaller than this one – but they can be bigger too. A couple of years ago in Cornwall a pair of divers swam with one of these that was bigger than they were. And…" she paused impressively, "once you see a jellyfish, you should always keep an eye out." She turned back to scan the water again as the jellyfish slid away from them down into the depths. "Jellyfish are a leatherback turtle's favourite food."

Grandpa frowned at her. "I'm sure we don't get turtles in Wales," he said, although he didn't sound that certain.

"I promise you we do!"

"Saw one last week," Pete called smugly from
the controls at the back of the boat. "Huge.
Swimming along without a care in the world."

"Leatherbacks are the largest species of turtle,"
Alice told them. "They can weigh the same as
a small car – and they absolutely *love* jellyfish.
They come here to feed on them in the summer.
So definitely watch out!"

Everyone was silent as Pete sped the
Mermaid up again, watching closely for more
jellyfish, or car-sized turtles. Alice kept scanning
around with her binoculars, and Lillie noticed
her training them on a group of large seabirds
a little further out from the land. She waved to
Pete and pointed, and he turned the *Mermaid*
out to sea.

"What is it?" Lillie asked hopefully, and

everyone turned to look at Alice.

"Those are gannets out there – they're the biggest seabirds we get in the UK and they're beautiful just in themselves, especially when they're fishing and diving down to the water – they're so incredibly fast. But we're actually heading out to check if they're chasing dolphins."

Lillie gasped and Alice nodded, smiling at her. "They're really clever, gannets. They let dolphins do a lot of the work for them, stirring up the fish and herding them into a shoal, and then they come along behind and snatch them out of the water. So if we spot gannets fishing, it's always worth going a bit closer to see if there are dolphins too."

Lillie crossed her fingers tightly as the boat cruised towards the circling gannets.

The jellyfish had been amazing, and a surprise, but it was dolphins she really wanted to see.

As they came closer, it was easier to see just how big the gannets were. There were more of them now, gliding round and round, and occasionally swooping down with a loud, excited cackle to snatch a fish. Then they would circle, swimming on the surface before launching into the air to dive again.

"Definitely something there bringing the fish up," Alice murmured. "Oh yes, look!"

Lillie squinted eagerly towards the water – and there they were. A smooth grey back curved out of the sea, and then just a flick of a darker tail. She felt her mum take in a huge, delighted breath beside her, and she slipped her hand into Mum's, squeezing tight.

"Oh, there's more of them!" Lara whispered

from the row in front.

"Four, I think," Alice said. "One of them's smaller, maybe a mother and her calf."

They watched intently for as the gannets dived into the water around the dolphins. Then the feeding frenzy slowed, the seabirds sliding away towards the cliffs again.

"Are the dolphins going?" Lillie breathed to Alice. She was half standing in her seat now, trying to get a better sight of those smooth, curving backs. What was it that made them so fascinating?

"I don't think so." Alice looked pleased with herself. "No, I think they've spotted us, actually. Just watch."

Lillie held her breath, gazing at the tiny, plinking waves. Alice was right. The dolphins had definitely noticed them.

They were arcing around, making their way back to the boat – it looked as though they wanted to swim alongside it.

"I'll start us up again," Pete called.

"Oh! Why?" Mum asked, sounding surprised. "Can't we stay and watch them for a while."

"Don't worry, we will," Alice explained. "If we get underway, they'll swim with us. They like to ride on our bow wave, or in the wake behind the boat – when we're cutting through the water. It makes a sort of current and the dolphins can hitch a lift."

The *Mermaid* eased away gently and Lillie watched as the dolphins pulled alongside. "Are they *playing*?" she asked Alice, and the wildlife guide nodded back to her.

"We think so! Scientists have done lots of research on it – whether dolphins use boats because it's faster and easier than just swimming to where they want to go, but no one's really sure. But I've seen them do it lots of times, and it really looks like they're having fun." She laughed. "I mean, look!"

One of the dolphins was up ahead of them now, bouncing along as the nose of the boat pushed the water into a wave. It was practically standing up in the water, balancing on its tail.

THE SUMMER DOLPHIN

It definitely looked to Lillie like the dolphin was having a good time. It seemed happy – and it made Lillie feel happy too. She knew that captive dolphins had been made to do tricks for years at water parks, balancing balls on their noses and jumping through hoops, but this seemed different. The dolphins were enjoying themselves, having fun with the boat. With them.

THE SUMMER DOLPHIN

Lillie gasped as one of the smaller ones turned on to its back, showing its lighter tummy. She could see the dolphin looking at her, she was sure of it. It had a pink nose – Lillie knew it wasn't a nose really, but whatever the bit at the end of a dolphin's snout was called.

That dolphin was smiling at her.

"Didn't you want to go rock-pooling with
Frankie and Lara?" Mum asked, frowning
a little at Lillie. "I love all those little creatures."

"I know." On their first beach trip, Lillie had
seen a few smaller rock pools at the edge of the
sand, where the rocks tumbled around the base
of the cliff. She'd loved the beadlet anemones,
waving their tiny dark red fronds. Lara and
Frankie had set off to walk round to the next
cove with Auntie Sasha – they could reach it at
low tide – apparently it had even bigger, better
pools to go searching in.

"You could probably catch Frankie and Lara up, if you hurried?" Mum peered at the narrow sandy path. "They've only just gone."

Lillie stared down at her feet, avoiding Mum's eyes. She'd asked Frankie if she could go with them. She'd hoped maybe Frankie would be feeling a bit guilty about the bedroom situation. After all, Lillie hadn't made a fuss about it! She could have told Mum or Gran about them stomping on her and being so mean. She could have pointed out that they were supposed to take turns having the proper beds. Auntie Sasha had said so! *That* hadn't happened. But she hadn't done anything to get Frankie and Lara into trouble. She'd just said there wasn't a lot of space on the floor and the window seat had looked comfy. Which it was. Gran had given her a thoughtful look when she'd explained at breakfast, but she hadn't said anything, except to offer Lillie more pillows. Grandpa had pointed out that the window seat was hollow underneath, so she could put her bags away inside it. It was like her own tiny room.

But when she'd seen them gathering buckets that morning, before everyone set off for the beach – a different beach this time – Lillie had forgotten for a moment that Frankie was hardly talking to her.

"Oh! Are you going to look for those little fish? In the rock pools? Can I come with you?"

This time Frankie hadn't even looked guilty for a second. She just said, "No," quite flatly. No word of explanation.

"But…"

"She said no, Lillie," Lara put in. "Don't beg, it's embarrassing. Run along now." And she'd smirked, a tiny, horrible little smile just lifting up one corner of her mouth.

Lillie ran along. And now she was the one stuck explaining to Mum. There was no point telling, she was quite sure of that. After all, what would Frankie and Lara do if Mum told them to be nice to poor little Lillie? They weren't suddenly going to have a personality transplant and actually let her join in. Although it did seem a bit like Frankie had changed as soon as Lara had turned up. Lillie was just hoping it wouldn't last when they got back home. She wasn't sure how she felt about her big sister right now. Even if Frankie was only being so nasty because of Lara, she could still have chosen not to, couldn't she? Clearly she wanted to be mates with Lara more than she wanted to stick up for Lillie.

"I wanted to stay here and watch for dolphins," she told Mum now, getting up from the picnic blanket. It was sort of true. Lillie couldn't get the wonderfulness of that half an hour when the dolphins danced around their boat out of her head.

"Oh, weren't they fab?" Mum said, smiling. "Your grandpa did well there, we were so lucky. Though…" She looked at the sea, glittering and silvery in the morning sunlight. "I'm not sure we'd see them from here, Lillie love. I think you might need to be out on a boat."

"I might," Lillie said stubbornly. It was her excuse and she was sticking to it. "They do come and swim with people sometimes. I looked it up on your phone. It was on the website for the local paper."

"OK…" Mum leaned over and gave her a hug. "Shout if you see them."

Lillie hadn't told Mum the whole truth about the newspaper article. It had been from the local paper, but the dolphin had been a regular at a different beach, not too far away. He'd been on his own and he'd been really curious about people. He'd come in close to the beach and he wanted to play. He swam around people, popping up next to them, standing on his tail, getting excited and bouncy – like a toddler, one of the marine scientists had said. So many people had come to the beach to try and catch a glimpse of him, or even swim with him – a wild creature who seemed to love humans – there was something rare and magical about it.

The problem was, even though the dolphin was young and friendly, he was big – really big, big enough to be dangerous without realizing it. If he'd knocked into someone swimming, they could have been badly injured, had bones broken. The dolphin wouldn't have meant any harm, he just didn't understand how fragile humans were in the water. A marine rescue team had ended up coaxing him away from the beach because the local authorities had been so worried someone was going to get hurt.

That all made sense to Lillie. Obviously a huge dolphin whose natural element was water, and who had been born swimming, would find it hard to understand how delicate humans could be.

But she was still standing at the edge of the water, gazing out at the silver surface of the sea, and hoping to see the smooth grey curve of a dolphin's back. She wanted to get close. She wanted that moment again, when she had stared at the pink-nosed dolphin and the dolphin had gazed back, full of curiosity. Lillie knew it had been special and she was lucky to have had even that short encounter, but she couldn't help hoping for more.

She glanced across the beach at Mum, who was sitting in a camping chair and leaning over to look at something Gran was showing her.

"I'm just going to walk over there!" she yelled – waving vaguely along the beach.

"Not too far!" her mum called back after a tiny pause, which Lillie thought was her running through about six million different terrible things that could happen, and deciding that Lillie was probably sensible enough to be safe and not get carried out to sea by enormous jellyfish or leatherback turtles or gannets the size of aeroplanes.

Lillie nodded and waved and pottered off along the edge of the water, sighing happily to herself. She minded about Frankie, of course

she did, but actually it was quite special to be
by herself somewhere so wonderful. This beach
was an Area of Outstanding Natural Beauty –
there were signs everywhere telling you so. Lillie
could see why. It was huge, and even though it
was the summer holidays and there were loads
of people, it still felt open and almost empty.
There was so much sky and sea, and it made
Lillie feel as if she was a tiny little speck of a
person somewhere in between. It was reassuring.
As if Frankie and Lara couldn't really be that
important, not when all this was here.

There were quite a few people in the sea,
either swimming or playing on bodyboards,
although it wasn't great surfing weather, the
sea was calm and the waves were hardly there
at all. Lillie padded on, walking through the
shallow ripples that washed over her feet,

each tiny wave a shock of cold.

She didn't really think she was going to see any dolphins. She kept looking though, just in case, gazing out to sea and frowning at each little bump of wave, in case it was a smooth grey back. Eventually Lillie looked over her shoulder and decided she could only just see her family's little camp of rugs and beach chairs, so she should probably go back before Mum and Dad went into a panic. It was harder to look at the sea on the way back, the sun was shining in her eyes and glittering the water, so every wave made her heart jump a little.

As she came closer, she could see that Mum was standing up now, shading her eyes so she could gaze along the beach. Lillie waved, just once, to show that she knew, she was coming, everything was OK. She hadn't been eaten by

a jellyfish. Mum beamed at her, waved, and then
sat down as if she hadn't been fussing at all.

And then Lillie looked at the water again,
and a pod of dolphins looked back at her.
She was so surprised that she spoke to them.
"You came back," she said out loud, her eyes
widening. "You really came back!"

Lillie stood there in the shallows with
a huge, wide smile, beaming at the dolphins

as they dipped in and out of the water, gradually
coming closer and closer. It was four of them
again – surely it had to be the same four? They
leaped up out of the water and arced across
the surface together, like dancers following
their music. A creamy ripple of white foam
broke around them each time they dived back
under the surface. It was so beautiful that Lillie
laughed. She was just so happy to see them.

Then one of the dolphins broke the pattern, swimming out in front of the others, its dark fin cutting through the water towards Lillie and the beach.

The dolphin swooped in and out of the water, its shining back appearing at the top of each curve, until it stopped, only thirty metres or so from the beach, gazing curiously towards Lillie. It was looking *at* her, Lillie was sure of it. It could see her. And it was the same one. That bright, inquisitive gaze, the pinkish nose. It was the dolphin who had watched her on the boat trip.

Forgetting that she was still wearing shorts and a T-shirt, and ignoring the excited chatter as other holidaymakers along the beach began to notice the dolphins, Lillie started to walk into the sea towards the pink-nosed dolphin.

She hardly even
noticed the chill
of the water, she
just wanted to
get closer. Lillie
squeaked
in delighted
surprise as the
dolphin arced up
out of the water,
only a few metres
ahead of her. She
caught a glimpse of
its blowhole, and the
dark, intelligent eye
as it dived back under
the surface.

"Lillie! Get back here!"

THE SUMMER DOLPHIN

Lillie blinked, all of a sudden remembering that there were other people on the beach, that it wasn't just her and the dolphin. She glanced behind her and saw Dad, racing up the beach, angling into the water towards her, still calling anxiously. The dolphin spotted him too and veered away suddenly, back out to sea. Lillie stretched out her hand without even thinking, almost as if she could touch it and ask it to come back – but of course it was gone already, disappearing into the waves.

"Lillie, what were you thinking?" Dad sounded horrified.

Lillie stared back at him, unsure how to answer. She didn't understand what he meant. How could she not have walked into the water? The dolphin had come to see her. It had been waiting for *her*.

Dad had caught up with her now and he grabbed her by the shoulders, turning her this way and that as if he wanted to make sure she was definitely in one piece. "Are you OK? It didn't bite you?"

"Of course not!" Lillie shook her head.

"Don't say it like that, Lillie! It's a wild creature, it could have hurt you!"

"But I was only going to say hello," Lillie whispered as Dad pulled her along, splashing through the shallows back to the beach where

Mum and Grandpa were waiting – and
Frankie and Lara. Gran and everyone else were
hurrying along the beach towards them too.
"It was the same dolphin we saw before, on the
boat trip. It had a pink nose. It remembered
me, I know it did."

Mum hugged Lillie tight as she stepped
out of the water, wrapping her up and almost
lifting her off her feet.

"There's no need to get upset, Bella,"
Grandpa murmured. "I'm sure Lillie wasn't
in any danger. Lots of people swim with
dolphins, you know."

"Don't encourage her!" Mum glared at him
over Lillie's head.

"It was OK, Mum," Lillie tried to say. She was
trying not to think about that newspaper article,
about the young dolphin who'd had to be moved

away from a beach to stop him accidentally hurting people. What she'd done was the same, but – she'd been sure she was safe. The pink-nosed dolphin hadn't been leaping around wildly like the one in the article. It had waited there in the water for her.

"Lillie, you need to stay with an adult," Mum said. "No going off on your own, do you hear me?"

Lillie heard a snort behind her – a nasty little snicker – and she knew it was Lara. She was about to protest, to say she hadn't done anything wrong – but something in Mum's face made her stay silent.

"What are we doing today?" Lillie asked.
They were into the second week of their holiday
now, and everyone was sitting round the huge
table in Gran and Grandpa's kitchen. It just
about fitted them all, if no one minded an
occasional elbow in the ribs. Gran had made
eggy bread for breakfast, and Lillie was halfway
through her third slice and slowing down.

"I thought a walk," Mum suggested brightly.
Frankie groaned and then went a bit pink
when everyone turned to look at her.

"It's just a bit hot for walking," she murmured.

"I know what you mean," Mum agreed. "But this walk is right by the sea, so it should be fresher. And I think the weather's cooling down a bit too – it's the start of September now."

Lillie sighed. As soon as they finished their holiday with Gran and Grandpa, it would be straight back to school. Only another few days. It wasn't that she didn't like school, it just seemed like such a big change after six weeks of summer holidays, of getting up late and wearing whatever she liked.

"Anyway, this walk's really special," Mum went on enthusiastically. "Do you remember when we went on the boat trip, and Alice and Pete showed us Worm's Head, the island you can walk out to at low tide? Where all the seabirds nest?"

"I thought it was protected," Gran said, frowning. "It's a nature reserve, isn't it?

I don't think you can walk there."

Mum nodded. "Not when the birds are nesting – but it opens up again at the end of August. So we're fine to walk over there now. I've checked the tides, and if we have an early lunch and set off after that, we'll time it just right. We've got to be careful. I don't want us getting stuck out there on a rocky island."

"I'd be all right," Lara said smugly. "I'm a really good climber. We went climbing down a waterfall on our Scout camp."

Lillie rolled her eyes at her plate. Lara always had to be better than everyone else. How was climbing down a waterfall meant to help if you were marooned on an island? She caught a disgusted expression on Charlie's face as well – she had a feeling he wasn't that impressed with their cousin either.

Mum eyed Lara thoughtfully. "I don't think there's a waterfall on Worm's Head, sorry, Lara. But it's very beautiful and dramatic, with huge cliffs, and one part of the path is over a natural rock bridge. There'll still be some seabirds, I expect, and there are seals as well. I'd love to see those. We didn't get to see any on the boat trip – I'm not complaining, I know it was only because we did a detour to watch the dolphins instead. But apparently there's a colony of seals that live on the rocks around Worm's Head, so it would be a great chance to spot them."

Lillie nodded eagerly. She'd seen seals at the zoo, but never a wild one, and she really wanted to. This holiday was turning into an amazing wildlife-spotting expedition.

In the end, after lunch Leon and Charlie decided to head down to the nearby beach by themselves – Leon's ankle was mostly better but he wasn't quite sure he could manage a long walk, and Gran said she'd stay because she had plans for something delicious and complicated for dinner. Everyone else set out on the walk – Lara and Frankie went off in front. Lara had been making a big thing of all the hiking trips she'd been on with Scouts, and how she was faster than everyone else, and fitter, and loved climbing... Frankie didn't, or not as far as Lillie knew, but obviously she wasn't going to say so.

Worm's Head was close to the beach where Lillie had seen the dolphins again the day before – the walk out across the causeway started from the cliffs above the beach. It wasn't that far from the village where Gran and Grandpa's house was, but Mum had suggested they drive there and park in the car park. Even just the bit out on to the island was a rocky, scrambly sort of walk and she didn't want to wear everybody out.

They set off from the car park, the wind

catching in everyone's hair and blowing away
some of the heat. Lillie ambled along, enjoying
the cool breeze on her arms and vaguely
listening to Grandpa telling Mum and Dad
and Uncle Dave and Auntie Sam about the
plans he and Gran had for their new garden.
Auntie Sasha was talking to Lara about
something, and Lillie found that Frankie
was walking beside her.

"Hey…" she murmured. It felt weird.
She'd hardly spoken to her sister this holiday.

"You OK?" Frankie asked, and Lillie didn't
answer her. It didn't sound as if Frankie
expected her to say how she really was.
It was just a thing you said…

Frankie slung an arm around her shoulders
and Lillie blinked, surprised for a moment.
Then she relaxed, leaning against Frankie's side.

Her sister smelled of body spray and washing powder and Lillie suddenly realized how much she'd missed her.

Then Lara came dashing past, grabbed Frankie's hand and pulled her away from Lillie, racing down the path. Lillie was left stumbling behind them.

"Oh, that was silly of Lara. Are you OK, Lillie?" Auntie Sasha hurried up, catching her arm. "You nearly fell over. I don't know what she was thinking!"

She's jealous. Lillie didn't say it, but she wanted to. Lara had decided she wanted Frankie all to herself, and Frankie loved being someone's favourite.

Instead, she just shrugged and ran over to Mum, who was looking at a noticeboard with Grandpa. Mum had that expression on her face that suggested she was trying not to argue. Lillie hadn't noticed it before this holiday, because she'd never really thought of her grandparents actually being Mum's mum and dad. They were just Gran and Grandpa – but of course they hadn't always been. Mum and Grandpa definitely rubbed

each other up the wrong way sometimes.
The face Mum was making reminded Lillie
of Frankie. It was the face of someone whose
parent was being decidedly annoying.

The noticeboard was headed "High and Low
Tides", and it had a list of days and times on it.
Lillie remembered what Mum had explained
about the causeway. This was how you worked
out when it was safe to walk to the island,
without getting trapped by the tide coming
in on your way back.

"Loads of time!" Grandpa was saying.
"You needn't have made your mother rush
lunch. We could have left much later."

Mum's lips had thinned, but she caught Lillie
looking at her and tried to smile and pretend
she wasn't cross. Lillie grinned at her, and Mum
smiled a real smile back. Grandpa was definitely

the sort of person who would get caught by
a rising tide, Lillie reckoned. He was so
optimistic and he always assumed that
things would work out just fine. Growing up
with Grandpa might be why Mum liked to
make sure they arrived ten minutes early for
absolutely everything. With a raincoat.
And an emergency snack.

"I'm a slow walker," she told Grandpa.
"Mum knows that. She says I have to stop and
look at everything. And if there are seals we're
all going to want to stop, aren't we?"

"Mmmm, maybe you're right." Grandpa
nodded. "Anyway, why are we all hanging
around here? Let's get on with this walk!"

Lillie saw her mum roll her eyes, and tried
hard not to laugh.

The causeway was one of those places that

made you realize how old the earth was,
Lillie decided, as they began scrambling
across the huge pale rocks at the very
beginning. They were streaked with dark
cracks and looked as though there might
be clutches of dinosaur eggs buried in the
hollows between them. They picked their way
over them on to a pebbly path scattered with
rock pools. Lillie darted away to investigate
one deep-looking one, crouching down to
peer into the miniature underwater world.
Tiny red beadlet anemones flickered their
fronds and Lillie was sure she saw a fish,
so small and thin it was almost transparent,
shooting into a crack between two rocks.
A dark green crab, no bigger than her
thumbnail, skittered over the pebbles just
in front of her foot.

"Any worms, Lillie?" Grandpa asked, leaning
over to look too.

"Only a fish and a little crab, and some
anemones. Oh, there's a top shell." She pointed
out the delicately striped shell, almost hidden
between two pebbles.

"It isn't that kind of worm," Mum said.
"It's old Norse – *wurm*." She said it with
a sort of accent, so it sounded like "vurrrm".
"It means dragon. The Vikings who named
it thought that the whole island looked like

a dragon, or maybe a sea serpent, sleeping
in the water."

Lillie frowned, trying to remember what
the island had looked like from the cliff, and
from the sea when they were on the boat trip.
It wasn't very dragon-y, as far as she could see.
But maybe, from the right angle…

"Imaginative lot, those Vikings." Grandpa
nodded.

"And I'm not sure exactly where it is,
but apparently there's a hole in the rocks
that splutters and roars when it's stormy,"
Mum added. "You can see why that would
make them think of a dragon." She looked
thoughtful. "I think if I was living here
a thousand years ago, when there was no
electric light, just candles and burning torches,
and it was cold and dark and stormy, I might

tell a story about a huge dragon sleeping
next to my village. Especially if I thought the
dragon might wake up and be on my side if
there was a battle." She glanced around at the
water lapping at the edge of the causeway.
"Come on. You know what I'm like – I really
don't want us to take too long and get stuck.
You can't just wade back across the causeway
once the tide comes in, you know. The sea
rushes in very quickly, and the currents are
really strong. It's a dangerous place to swim."

"Oh wow, look at this!" Dad called from
a little further up the causeway. "Hey, I've
found a shipwreck!"

Lillie scrambled over to him, and so did
Mum and the others, and Dad waved proudly
at a huge rusted anchor just sitting there half
buried among the pebbles.

"Oh, this was in my guidebook!" Mum looked delighted. "It's all that's left of the wreck of the *Samuel*, a coal ship that ran aground on the rocks about a hundred and forty years ago."

"What happened to the people on the ship?" Lillie asked anxiously.

"The coastguard spotted the ship's lights too close to the shore and realized that they were about to run aground," Mum told her. "They threw a rope to the ship somehow. I don't know how they did that! Anyway, they managed to rescue the crew by getting them to cling on to the rope."

Lillie crouched down to touch the pitted, rusty metal and shivered. It didn't seem like much to be left of a whole ship. She was glad the crew had made it away safely.

"It's a bit eerie, isn't it?" Mum said, taking

her hand, and Lillie nodded.

"Will all of this be underwater when the tide comes in?" she asked, looking around the pebbly causeway as they walked on. The island rose up in front of them, covered in wiry green turf and golden gorse bushes. Actually, the grass and bright yellow patches of flowers did make it look more dragon-ish, especially with the scaly rocks poking out here like a sharp, ragged spine.

"Uh-huh. And I think it's quite deep as well," Mum said. "Now we can go up over the top of this bit for a really good view." She started picking her way between the rocks and everyone else followed her, strung out in single file along the dragon's back.

"Where's the bit with the bridge?" Frankie called as she clambered up on to the top of the first lump of dragon.

"It's part of the Middle Head, I think." Mum shaded her eyes, looking along the island. "We've got to do some more scrambly rocks before we get there. This is why I wouldn't let you wear flip-flops," she added to Frankie, who made a face back at her.

"OK, you were right…"

Lillie had thought they'd already done the scrambly bit getting up on to the island, but it turned out that was the easy bit. The rocks of the Low Neck were strange, toothy things, almost like lots of layers squashed together sideways. They were sun-warmed, and spotted here and there with patches of yellow lichen and tiny tufts of grass. Luckily the rocky patch was still high enough to stay out of the water so it wasn't too slippery to cross. Everyone was looking down at their feet, though, and concentrating, so nobody spotted the next part of the walk until Mum pointed it out.

"*This* is Devil's Bridge," Mum called back to Frankie, grinning as proudly as if she'd put it there herself.

"Oh wow…" Lillie whispered. "Are we walking across *that*?"

It was those same squashed layers of rock – but this time they were squashed together over a gap, with a dark channel of sea frothing below.

"Are you sure this is safe, Mum?" Frankie asked, eyeing the bridge suspiciously as they headed over the grass towards it. Lillie could see why she was doubtful – the bridge did look quite fragile.

Mum waited until they were in the middle of it before stopping to peer over the edge. Lillie looked over too, but then very quickly looked away again. It seemed a very long way down and she didn't like the way the water was foaming and splashing underneath them.

"Apparently this is actually a collapsed sea cave," Mum said. "Geologists expect this bit will collapse too, one of these days."

"Bella!" Auntie Sasha glared at her.
"Why are you telling us this when we're
in the middle of it?"

"Well, for fun really…"

Lillie scurried over the rest of the bridge on to the last part of the island, and sat down, feeling as though she wanted more of her to be connected to solid ground. She wound her fingers into a clump of pink flowers springing out of the tufty grass and held on tight.

"Are you scared, Lillie?" Lara asked, smirking a little. "I love stuff like this. But then I don't mind heights."

"No," Lillie growled back. "I'm fine." Then she frowned and stood up, pointing back across the bridge to the Inner Head. "Hey! Look down there! Mum, are those the seals?"

Lillie almost forgot about the sea surging below as she hurried back over the bridge to get a better look. They'd come over the top of the Outer Head and hadn't spotted the seals, but now she could see there was a path round

the side of the island, and there on the seaweedy rocks below were three plump seals, gazing up at them with huge, round eyes.

"Oh, I'm so happy we saw them," Mum whispered, putting her arm around Lillie. "Aren't they gorgeous?"

"They're a bit funny-looking, Mum," Frankie said. "It's as if someone blew them up with a pump. But they are cute."

"They've got faces quite like dogs, I think," Lillie said, peering down. "Such a lot of whiskers. But no ears, or at least you can't see them. Oh!" She laughed as one of the seals obviously decided it didn't like being talked about and shuffled off across the rocks to dive into the sea.

They crouched on the path, watching the seals for a while longer – even Lara decided she wasn't bothered about doing the last bit of the walk to the Outer Head and climbing up the ninety-metre-high rocks at the very end of the island. The seals were more exciting. But eventually Dad pointed out that they should head back before the tide turned and Mum sprang up at once, looking worried.

"I nearly forgot!"

"There's loads of time," Dad said soothingly.

"But I reckon we should set off now to
be safe."

The scramble back over the spiky rocks of
the Low Neck was harder this time, now that
they were tired and just the tiniest bit worried
about the tide. As they reached the causeway
it was clear they had plenty of time, though.
The tide was starting to come in – Mum said
she was sure there were patches of pebbles
they'd seen on the way that were underwater
now. But there was still a clear, wide path
back to the mainland.

Lillie stopped to look behind her after they'd
crossed the causeway, trying to see the tide
coming in. The path definitely looked narrower.
A couple of walkers they'd spotted ahead of
them up on the Outer Head were hurrying
back.

THE SUMMER DOLPHIN

"Come on, Lillie! We're going to get ice creams!" Frankie called, and Lillie turned to go. But just as she was about to race after everyone else, she caught a movement in the water – a beautiful, dipping, rocking motion that was wonderfully familiar.

The dolphins were back.

Lillie drew in a breath to shout, to point them out – but then she didn't. She just watched silently, as the dolphins cut through the water, all in line. She was sure that they knew she was there.

Lillie kept thinking back to that moment with
Frankie on their walk, where they'd felt like
real sisters again. She was loving this holiday –
all the amazing creatures to spot, the hot sun,
swimming in the sea, spending time with Gran
and Grandpa – how could she not? But she'd
missed having Frankie there as her big sister,
someone she knew she could count on.

The next morning no one seemed to have
a plan for the day – it was cooler, a little
bit grey, not an ideal beach day. Gran had
mentioned a lovely old house to visit,

but there was no rush. Everyone was pottering around, taking it easy.

Now was the time to talk to Frankie, Lillie decided. She just needed to get her away from Lara, which was easier said than done. The pair of them seemed to hide out in the attic bedroom the whole time. Lillie curled up on her window seat with a book, watching out. Frankie was bound to need the loo sometime, wasn't she? The bathroom was on Lillie's floor, so she could catch Frankie on her way there.

Lillie had just got to a really good bit of the book and she almost missed the creak of the attic stairs. Then Frankie appeared and she jumped up to catch her.

"Lillie! Were you hiding?"

"I was just reading my book…" Lillie

shrugged, trying to look natural. "You OK?"

Frankie eyed her suspiciously. "I'm all right. What are you making that face for?"

"I'm not making a face!" Lillie sighed. "I just – I wanted to talk to you."

Frankie glanced around, suddenly shifty. "What about?"

"I miss you." Lillie swallowed, hoping that her sister wasn't going to laugh. "Now that you're sharing a room with Lara, I don't get to see you, that's all. It was nice yesterday, when you walked with me," she added huskily.

"Oh, Lills…" Frankie started to say – but then there was a crashing of footsteps on the stairs and Lara appeared. Their cousin must have jumped the last few steps, Lillie reckoned. She darted out like a whirlwind, sweeping Frankie up.

"Come on!"

"But – where are you going?" Lillie asked, trying hard not to whine.

"Lillie, just leave us alone," Lara snapped. "Stop pestering us!"

"Oh, hey…" Frankie murmured weakly, but that was all.

"I'm not pestering," Lillie said, folding her arms and glaring back at them. "I just wanted to spend some time with my sister, that's all. How come it's not allowed all of a sudden? She doesn't belong to you, you know."

Lara snorted with confident laughter. "Don't be such a baby, Lillie. No one wants you around, just face it." She didn't even look at Frankie – she was completely sure that Frankie wasn't going to protest. And she didn't.

"Frankie, please!" Lillie hurried after them as Lara led Frankie off towards the stairs – actually pulling her along. "I just wanted to talk to you."

Her sister whirled round on the top step. "Didn't you hear what Lara said? Go away! No one wants their babyish little sister hanging around all the time!"

Lara laughed again and the two of them clattered away down the stairs, leaving Lillie leaning against the wall, trying not to cry with fury.

She was going to show them. That was all
Lillie could think, it was repeating over and
over inside her head. She'd show them. She'd
make them see. She wasn't a baby and they
were going to know it. Somehow.

Lillie crept down the stairs as quietly as she
could. She wasn't sure what her plan was,
she needed time to work it out, but she knew
she had to get out of the house, away from
Frankie and Lara. They were in the kitchen.
She could hear them talking to Gran. Lillie
sucked in a breath as she accidentally knocked
Frankie's hoodie, hanging on the end of the
stairs. Her sister's phone was in the pocket
and it clunked loudly against the banisters,
but no one seemed to have heard.

Lillie was just about to open the front door and slip out, when an idea struck her and she smiled. Frankie's phone was quite new and she loved it. Her sister was always messaging friends and she spent hours on TikTok. It was pretty amazing she'd been without the phone long enough to leave it in her hoodie, to be honest. She'd make Frankie panic, serve her right.

Lillie tiptoed back to the stairs and grabbed the phone – in the purple glitter snow-globe case that Frankie had saved up for – and then shot out of the door.

In the back of her head she remembered Mum saying that she mustn't go off on her own, but she was too angry to care.

As she hurried up the lane away from Gran and Grandpa's house, Lillie glanced over towards the sea, glittering a pale, silvery blue in the morning sun. Four dark marks cut across the water, little commas. The dolphins.

And all at once Lillie knew where she was going.

When she came to the headland, there were already a couple of families bustling around in the car park, making sure they had bottles of water and arguing about sun cream. Lillie felt strange for a moment. Seeing them squabbling and laughing together made her realize she was all on her own, even though that was the point – she wanted to be alone! She was going to walk all the way to the tip of Worm's Head and climb that high outcrop of rocks, where not even Lara had been. She was going to do it by herself and take photos on Frankie's stolen phone to prove it, and *then* let them try and call her a baby.

The dolphins had shown her the way.

The two families set off down the path to the

causeway just a little apart, and Lillie realized she'd been lucky, arriving at the same time they did. Other walkers might have worried about a nine-year-old girl doing this trip on her own, they'd think she was too young (of course she wasn't, that's what she was trying to prove). There was supposed to be a volunteer on duty in the coastguard hut too, watching out to make sure no one was setting off down the causeway too late, or had got hurt and stuck on the island maybe. But if she could be a little bit sneaky and careful, and stay somewhere in between those two families, not too close to either one, everyone would just assume she belonged with the others. It was perfect.

She strolled down the causeway after them, hoping she'd be able to lose them all once they were on the island – there were different

paths around and across, and all those huge
boulders and strange channels and layers
of rock. She could hide away, maybe. She
wanted to have the island to herself. Just for
a little bit.

The children from both the other families
were investigating the rock pools, which was
fine with Lillie. She headed round the side
of a larger rock, where she'd be almost hidden,
and sat down cross-legged at the edge of a pool,
tiny but deep. It was her first moment to pause,
and breathe, and wonder about what she'd done.
She was going to be in so much trouble when
she went home. Lillie sighed, trailing her fingers
in the chilly water. She could go back now,
and maybe no one would have missed her.
She might be able to say that she'd been down
at the end of the garden, or – or asleep and

she hadn't heard anyone calling. She could, just possibly, get away with it.

But did she want to?

Lillie shook her head firmly at a hermit crab that was creeping across the pebbled bottom of the pool. It would be worth getting into trouble, to see the look on Lara's face when she told them she'd been all the way to the top of those rocks. And she'd have the photos on Frankie's phone to prove it. Lillie carefully patted her shorts' pocket to make sure the phone was still there. However cross she was with Frankie, she didn't want anything to happen to her sister's phone. And if Lara called her a baby again, Lillie would be able to look down her nose and remember how brave she'd been. Intrepid, that was the word. Even if it didn't shut Lara up, Lillie would know.

Voices were moving away again. Lillie peered
carefully around the rock. If she kept going,
she needed to set off now — or she could stay
watching the water, then creep back to Gran
and Grandpa's and pretend that everything was
fine and she hadn't been gone at all.

Lillie didn't even stop to think.

It was more fun exploring the island by herself. Both the families had gone on ahead and Lillie was pretty sure that the coastguard volunteers with their binoculars wouldn't be able to spot her now. If she stayed around the west side of the island, she'd be hidden by the tall cliffs.

Now that she didn't have Mum chasing her on, she could stop to admire the wild surfaces of the rocks, some of them streaked with red, almost as if the stones were bleeding. There were strange little pockmarks here and there, and she pressed her fingers into them, imagining the sea dragon scratching his scales. It was sunnier now and the rocks were warm. Lillie climbed up on to a fat boulder and leaned against the rock face, closing her eyes and listening to the waves. They were crashing loudly all around the island but they soon settled into a soothing background rush and pull. She could pick out the occasional sharp cry of a seabird, and laughter and yelps from the walkers further ahead. She needed to remember to stay out of their way, Lillie thought dreamily.

A strange sound, like a coughing bark, woke her out of a half dream and Lillie stared around. She couldn't believe she'd nearly fallen asleep! Then again, it did make sense. She'd been so upset with Frankie and Lara, and then she'd set off on a longish walk… Mum always said that emotions wore you out.

But what had that noise been? Lillie gazed around, blinking away her sleepiness, and then caught her breath. Only a few steps away from her, tucked among the boulders, was a seal, lying on its side and staring back at her rather suspiciously. It was quite a long way from the water's edge and Lillie wondered if it was stuck. It certainly looked as if it would have a hard time struggling back across the rocks to the water.

Had it been there all the time, while she'd been climbing around looking at the rocks? How could she have missed it? The seal wriggled clumsily over on to its front, still eyeing Lillie, and she saw it settle back into its spot between two large rocks – almost completely camouflaged. The mottled grey-white of its fur made it nearly impossible to spot, even though Lillie knew it was there. Its claws were out, Lillie noticed, her eyes widening. Great, scythe-like curved claws that she absolutely did not want to get anywhere near. She must have really scared it.

"Sorry…" she whispered. "I'll leave you alone. You're safe here, till the water comes back. I won't tell anyone. I'd never even have noticed you if you hadn't made that barking noise."

She backed away slowly, scrambling between

the rocks and up on to the grassy path across
the Inner Head. The two families had moved
on now, she realized happily. Lillie was all
alone on the island. She stretched and took
a deep breath of the salty, seaweedy air.
Then she set off to Devil's Bridge, determined
that this time she wasn't going to scurry across
without looking down. She was brave and
determined, Lillie told herself. She was going
on her own adventure. She stopped to breathe
again just before she stepped on to the stone
bridge, looking around her at the sky and sea,
the sea just a darker shade of blue, streaked
with cloud-like wave foam.

She kept looking down at the water around
her as she walked across, feeling the sea wind
catch her hair. She felt protected – lifted up –
ready for the walk across the Outer Head to

the tall rocks at the very tip of Worm's Head.
Lillie took a couple of photos from the bridge
and then set off across the thin, grassy skin that
stretched over the worm's rocky spine.

Mum had said that the rocks at the tip were
difficult to climb, and as Lillie looked up
at them she thought *difficult* was probably an
understatement. How was she ever supposed
to get up there?

But after looking for a little while she began
to see that there were places to put her hands
and feet, little cracks and lumps of rock to grab
on to. She could do it, she told herself. If Lara
could manage all that rock climbing, then so
could she. She started to scramble up the rocks,
catching her breath a couple of times as her
feet skidded, pressing herself against the rock
wall like the barnacles far below. Lillie was sure

THE SUMMER DOLPHIN

she could feel the waves striking rock –
the rhythm thudded through her, thumping
like a heartbeat. Then she squeaked out loud
as a heavier wave crashed against the island
and water shot up the side of the rocks, a fine
spray catching her cheek. The blowhole!

Lillie was starting to understand why the Vikings had called the island a "wurm". The pulsing beat of the waves made it feel alive under Lillie's fingers. She could almost sense the dragon breathing under that thin skin of rock and grass and lichen. She was just waiting for it to move, for the long, coiling back to twist and loop out of the water. It would dive down, deep, deep into the sea, carrying Lillie with it, and the seals and the tiny creatures from the rock pools…

She was almost at the very tip of the Worm's Head now. Lillie struggled up to stand on top of the rocks, and gasped. She hadn't expected the view to be so incredible. She could see all the way back along the worm to the mainland, and the golden curve of sand that was Rhossili Bay. Carefully, she took out

Frankie's phone to take pictures, so she could prove she'd made it all the way. She took a video too, holding out the phone and spinning slowly round to get the full view.

It was as she was lingering on the sunny water, pointing the phone straight out to sea, that she caught the dolphins leaping out across the surface again.

They skipped over the water like skimmed
stones – Grandpa had been trying to teach her
and the boys the night before. Held up by the
sea wind, Lillie could sense a little of their wild
surge through the water. She laughed out loud
with the joy of it. They were back – they'd come
to find her again!

She watched them fishing for a while, taking more photos as the gannets arrived again, diving down to snatch the fish the dolphins had helpfully herded in. Then the dolphins streamed away in a line together, disappearing under the water and leaving Lillie to catch her breath.

And her thoughts. She hadn't been thinking, not for ages. Not since she'd woken from her half-sleep and seen the seal watching her. It had been wonderful, to stop thinking, to stop worrying about her sister and how strange and sad everything was. It felt like a horrible weight had lifted away for a little while. Except she'd stopped thinking about everything else too, like the time … and the tide. What time was it?

With shaky fingers, Lillie turned the phone away from the sun's glare and looked at the clock display. Then she swallowed hard, closed her eyes

and opened them to look again, in case she'd
made a mistake and it was different. It had
to be different.

She should have set off back to the causeway
and the mainland over an hour ago.

Lillie shoved the phone into the pocket of
her hoodie and started to slip and scramble
recklessly back down the rocks, at one point
sliding a couple of metres on her bottom before
she fetched up with her feet caught against
a little ledge.

She sat there, gasping for breath, her heart skittering with fear. That had been so close. She needed to slow down. It was too dangerous to rush. But the tide! She couldn't wait – slow and careful was dangerous too. She pushed herself up from the tiny ledge and began to pick her way down again, her fingers trembling as she tried to steady herself. At last she reached the flatter ground of the Outer Head, and scurried along the spine of the worm, heading for Devil's Bridge again. Lillie hardly noticed the height above the water this time, or the white foam churning below. She was too focused on the way back – whether there would *be* a way back. What would happen if she was too late for the causeway? She couldn't stay out here on the island till the next low tide, it would be hours and hours! Mum and Dad would be panicking, she'd be in so much trouble.

And Frankie and Lara would laugh at her, for being stupid enough to get caught by the tide.

Lillie gritted her teeth together. That wasn't going to happen. She sped up again, dodging round the lichen-crusted stones, fixing her eyes on the low path ahead. The neck between the Outer Head and the Inner Head had shrunk to a narrow spit of rock with waves licking at either side. It looked nothing like it had earlier on. Lillie stopped for a moment, swallowing hard as she stared across. She hadn't known – she hadn't *imagined* – it would be like this. She hadn't really understood the tide at all.

Lillie forced herself to walk out across the Low Neck, her trainers slipping on the stones. She had to keep going down on to all fours to grip the strange, sharp, layered rocks. The Inner Head of the worm rose up in front of her, hiding the causeway. Lillie stared at the high hump of rock in front of her, panting wearily. She wasn't sure if it was quicker to go up and over or round. Would the path round the side even be above water now? Lillie shuddered and set off climbing again. The panic and adrenaline were making it hard to catch her breath properly, she could still feel her heart skittering, and the climb seemed to take forever. Her feet felt so heavy as she trudged across the top of the Inner Head, the last part of the island before the causeway.

There! She could see it. It was still there! Mostly, anyway. There were a few places where the water was lapping over the stones, but she didn't mind wet feet. It would be fine.

Lillie let out a gasping laugh of relief and hurried down between the sandy rocks, into the strange little sea-worn passage between the island and the causeway.

Lillie's heart thudded with relief as she set out
along the causeway, hopping from stone to
stone. The rock pools she'd been peering into
earlier had all disappeared now, swallowed
up by the sea. Only the larger rocks were left,
like stepping stones. Ahead of her, water had
already covered the very middle of the causeway
– where the land was lowest, Lillie supposed.
She'd get her feet soaked going over that bit,
but it couldn't be that deep.

She'd forgotten how long it took to go across
the causeway. The strange folds and channels

in the rocks made it more of a clamber than
a walk and she kept having to slow down and
pick her way across the more difficult bits.
She could see the level of the water rising with
each wave. They surged in and then sucked
slowly back – but every time there was a little
less of the causeway left. The water was lapping
closer at Lillie's feet.

She reached the flooded part of the causeway
sooner than she expected, despite it being
hard-going. It seemed to be there in front
of her quite suddenly as she struggled over
another slippery boulder. The tide had covered
more of the path, of course, Lillie realized,
feeling slightly sick as she stared at the dark
water beneath her feet. It was stretching
further across the causeway with every wave.
It was going to be hard to find her way across

the rocks when she couldn't see where she was putting her feet.

Lillie looked round behind her. She could go back… Wait on the island for low tide. It would be seven hours – that was what she and Mum had worked out when they'd looked at the tide tables pinned up on the board on the Outer Head. She could call Mum on Frankie's phone, so at least they'd know where she was.

"Don't be such a baby," Lillie told herself furiously. It was the thought of Frankie that spurred her on. She wasn't going to let her big sister know she'd been stupid enough to lose track of time – and that she'd crept back on to the island, too scared to get her feet wet.

Biting her bottom lip between her teeth, she stepped carefully into the water. It wasn't deep at all – it hardly came halfway up her trainers!

Lillie gave a nervous little laugh of relief, and took her next step, and then another, and another. It was OK! She was doing it, it was going to be fine!

And then her next step wasn't there.

Lillie plunged sideways, her arms flailing as she fought for balance. There was nothing to grab hold of – nothing to save her. She slammed down into the water, crumpled on to her side. Part of Lillie knew it couldn't be that deep, not yet, but it *felt* deep. Her face was underwater and she was struggling for breath. She swallowed a great gulp of seawater and retched, sitting up in the water, spluttering and spitting. Another wave washed over her, and Lillie could feel its strong pull. Another wave, and another – each one seemed to hit her harder, bumping her over the rocks hidden under the water.

She needed to get back on her feet, now, and over the causeway. She couldn't just sit here! But she was cold and wet and shivery, and it seemed so difficult to move. Lillie shook her head, and then grimaced as a wave of pain shot through her. She must have hit herself on a rock. Shakily she tried to feel for a bump or a cut, but she was too wet with seawater to tell if she was bleeding. Her fingers didn't come away bloody, at least.

Lillie pushed trembling hands down into the water, feeling for solid rock to help push herself up. She got to her feet and tried to walk on, but the water was knee-deep now and she could feel the power of the current, trying so hard to sweep her off her feet and send her sideways. She still felt dizzy too – she really must have hit her head, she thought vaguely. And had she lost time, somehow? The water seemed so much deeper than it had before. If she'd knocked herself out, perhaps she'd been sitting in the water for a while.

Lillie was pretty sure that the causeway

dropped lower in the middle. She wasn't at the deepest point, not yet. Was she even going to be able to stay on her feet? What if she was out of her depth in the next few steps? She turned round carefully, looking behind her, and her heart hammered. There was no path back to the island. It had disappeared already, hidden beneath a ruffled, glinting sea.

There was no way back – and only the faintest trace of a way forward. But she couldn't stand still. Lillie crept on, resisting the pull of the current as hard as she could, trying to hold herself upright in the water. The muscles in her chest and stomach were aching already as she tried to stand. The current was relentless, sucking and tugging.

Frankie's phone! Lillie glanced down in horror at her hoodie, the pocket underwater already. She hadn't even thought about it. She should have pulled the phone out and held it above her head, or something. Lillie made a face, realizing just how silly that was. There was no way she'd be able to keep the phone out of the water. It had probably been ruined the first time she fell in anyway. What she should actually have done was leave the phone on the island, if she wanted to keep it safe. Or she should have stayed on the island herself and used the phone to call for help. That would have been a much, much better idea, Lillie admitted to herself at last, as she gazed helplessly around at the causeway – which wasn't there.

Oh, she could see the ripples around a tiny point of rock here and there, and those dark shadows under the sparkling water, they had to be larger rocks. But the pathway itself had gone, slipped away so quickly under the fierce rush of the tide. She could still see the mainland, of course, with the coastguard's hut perched against the green hillside. She knew where she was aiming, but it looked more and more as though she was going to have to swim for it.

Frankie was going to be so angry, Lillie thought miserably as she felt around for the next step on to the rocks below her feet. Even though the water was clear, she couldn't see down far enough to place her steps and she kept slipping and wobbling. She just had to stay standing. Lillie gritted her teeth as the current dragged at her again, almost knocking her sideways this time. She caught her breath, panting with fear as the current eased a little and she could stop fighting for a moment.

She wouldn't be able to stand up against it for much longer. Lillie hurried to get a little further before the current tried to pull her off her feet again. The water was up to her chest now and she was having to reach down with her toes to touch the rocks. Even without the current, the salty seawater wanted her to float and it was hard to stay standing. Lillie stepped out again, and this time there was simply nowhere to put her foot – she stepped into nothingness. With a little yelp of panic she tried to backtrack. The wobbly ground of a moment before now seemed perfect and stable and wonderful, but it was no good. She flailed her arms, pushing away the water in a fury of splashing.

What was she supposed to do? They'd had a talk at school from someone at a lifesaving charity. They'd been shown a video in assembly. There were things you had to do if you were caught in deep water, Lillie knew there were. Special ways to keep safe – but she couldn't remember any of them.

She had a feeling she might have broken most of them already by being out in the middle of the sea on her own, in a place where she knew there were strong cross-currents and it was dangerous to swim.

Not panicking was probably one of the rules, but it was a bit late for that too.

Oh, she was supposed to kick off her shoes!

Lillie kicked wildly, but her trainers seemed to be glued to her feet. They didn't want to come off. She could feel that the current was getting stronger now – the water seemed to be churning around her, pulling her this way and that, but always further out and away from the shore.

Lillie looked around frantically, realizing how far away from the island she'd gone already.

She was beginning to understand that
she wouldn't be able to swim to shore.
The current was too strong, it wanted to
pull her sideways and she just couldn't swim
through it. Actually... Lillie gasped and shook
stinging salt water out of her eyes as a larger
wave crashed over her head. That was one of
the tips from the lifesaving talk. *Don't fight for
the shore.* Let the current carry you where it
wants to go, just stay calm and stay afloat.
By this time, the woman had explained, you
were unlikely to be able to rescue yourself.
You were waiting for the coastguard to send
a helicopter, or a lifeboat from the RNLI.
It was all about holding on until someone
else rescued you. *Stay afloat*, Lillie told herself,
gently scooping the water with her hands and
making slow kicks, as if she was jogging in

the sea. *Just stay afloat until they come for you.*

But no one knew that Lillie needed rescuing. Unless Frankie had noticed that her phone was missing, which she probably had by now, since it was practically glued to her hand, Dad said. Would they have worked out where Lillie had gone, though? Perhaps they were out looking for her around Gran and Grandpa's house. That wasn't anywhere near here. They did know how much Lillie loved the dolphins, though. They might have worked out that she'd gone to look for them again.

She should have left a note, Lillie thought miserably, feeling the ache in her arms and shoulders as she tried to carry on paddling and keep her head out of the water. She'd been so angry, she'd just walked out and

wanted them all to be sorry… Even Mum
and Dad and Gran and Grandpa, who hadn't
really done anything, except not see what was
going on.

Her legs were so tired too – if only she'd
been able to get her trainers off. It felt like
her feet had great blocks of cement stuck to
them. That was what gangsters did to get rid
of people, Lillie remembered, her thoughts
treacle-slow.

Swimming with the fishes…

Dad had told her about it.

She gasped and lurched out of the water
again. She'd nearly gone under! Lillie spat
out salt and coughed. She had to concentrate.
It was just that she was so cold, and it was
making her sleepy…

Lillie had just gone under for the second

time, when she felt something swish past
her in the water. It wasn't that anything
touched her, but she felt the water move.
She shook her head wearily and paddled
harder. She was imagining things. Maybe
the worm had woken up and come to help!
Lillie giggled and spluttered – and then
stared as a dolphin popped out of the water
in front of her, a dolphin with a definite
pinkish-grey nose. She was so surprised that
she stopped swimming entirely, and sank
again.

The dolphin shoved her out of the water
this time, the simplest way it could, by
swimming underneath her and pushing up.
Then it backed off a little and watched her,
as if it wasn't really sure what she was doing.
There was a curious, questioning look in its

dark eyes. Lillie had a feeling it thought she was a bit useless.

"You're right," she whispered, settling herself in the water again and trying to swim. "I was really stupid… Thanks for helping." That was what she meant to say, but it came out as a gargling splutter. She'd swallowed so much water and her throat was rough with coughing now.

The sight of the dolphin had given Lillie a little burst of energy, and she paddled harder for a minute or two while the dolphin swam on alongside, a metre or so away. It was keeping an eye on her, Lillie thought gratefully. It had already sorted her out once and it seemed interested now. The energy didn't last for long, though. Lillie was really tiring and every movement hurt. She couldn't feel her hands any more either.

The dolphin carried on swimming beside her, its fin breaking the surface every few seconds with a slurpy splash. It was getting closer, Lillie realized. Almost next to her now.

Then it brushed against her, its cool smooth skin slipping past and touching her cheek. It whistled at her, almost as if it wanted to tell her something.

"Are you trying to help?" Lillie murmured faintly. "I think you are…"

The dolphin circled round, gazing at her intently. Its eye was quite human, Lillie thought vaguely, the way it was set into little creases. They looked like eyelids. It had a kind face…

Lillie let go. Her hands were too cold and stiff to push against the water, and she was exhausted. It was just too hard to move. It was too hard even to think. Everything was sleepy and strange.

The dolphin was swimming around her again. It pushed her up out of the water, but slower this time, nudging her gently with that long, pinkish nose. "I can't play now," Lillie tried to tell it – and then she understood that it wasn't trying to play. It was lifting her up out of the water. It was trying to save her.

It wanted her to hold on.

Lillie's hands were still too numb to grip on tight, but the dolphin was swimming slowly. She managed to hook her arm around the dorsal fin sticking up from its back. Even just being a little more out of the water, with the sun shining on her, made Lillie feel more awake. Her fingers were tingling, as if the feeling was starting to come back, like pins and needles.

Where were they going? Lillie blinked, trying to wash the blurriness of seawater out of her eyes. Did the dolphin understand that

she needed to get out of the water? It was hard
to tell where it was taking her, she was still
too low in the choppy water to see. She could
feel the current sucking at her limbs – but
the dolphin's strong, beating tail could power
through it. Lillie wrapped her arm more tightly
around its fin, clinging on gratefully as they
cut through the water. Her arm ached, but
she wasn't letting go. The dolphin was making
squeaking, chittering noises – Lillie wasn't sure
if it was talking to her, or maybe to the others
in its pod. Were they close by? She thought
they always stayed together. She glanced
around, looking for more fins breaking the
surface, but she and the pink-nosed dolphin
seemed to be alone.

The water was settling, Lillie realized. The
churning boil of the current had slipped back

to something softer, sparklier. Little silver ripples on the surface, softly lapping as the dolphin carried her on. Had it brought them through the cross-current? Lillie shook her head and tried to focus. She still felt dazed with cold and exhaustion, but now she could

THE SUMMER DOLPHIN

see that they were coming towards a beach,
a great ring of golden sand, dotted with people.

People who were watching, and waving –
and one who was running into the water
towards her.

The dolphin slowed and Lillie felt her toes brush against the sea floor. She was back in her depth!

"Thank you," she whispered croakily, slipping her arm free. She patted her chill fingers gently against the dolphin's smooth skin. "Thank you for rescuing me."

The dolphin ducked down into the water and flicked up its tail fluke, splashing glittering spray over Lillie and making her laugh. Then it came up to sit with its head out of the water, watching her.

Watching to make sure she walked safely
on to the beach. It had known exactly what
she needed.

Lillie waded back through the water,
shivering as it got gradually shallower.
It was about knee-deep when Frankie
met her, flinging her arms around her and
hugging her tight. Lillie hugged her back,
closing her eyes as her sister's arms wrapped
her in warmth.

"Where have you been?" Frankie shouted,
breaking out of the hug and gripping Lillie's
arms, giving her a little shake. "I didn't know
where you were, you just disappeared and I was
so scared…"

"Were you?" Lillie blinked at her in
surprise.

"Of course I was."

Lillie glanced around, wondering where Lara was, since the two of them had been inseparable ever since the holiday started.

"Lara's back at the house," Frankie told her. She sounded a little ashamed, Lillie thought. "She said I was stupid, coming to look for you."

They stumbled out of the water together and sat down on the sand, just far enough up the beach that the little waves missed their toes. Lillie could hear people talking about the two girls who'd been in the water in their clothes, and had that really been a dolphin? But she didn't care. She watched the dolphin's fin cut away through the water, and flicked her fingers in a tiny, secret wave. A thank you.

"But how did you know that you needed to look for me anyway?" she asked, leaning against Frankie.

"No one knew where you were. I wanted to find you and say I was sorry. I thought you'd be with Gran, but she said she hadn't seen you. I don't know – something just felt wrong. And then I looked for my phone and it was gone. I knew I'd left it in my hoodie pocket. So I guessed you'd taken it."

"Frankie, it's gone," Lillie whispered. "It got wet, and then I lost it. I'm so sorry. I shouldn't have taken it."

Frankie snorted. "I kind of knew it wasn't going to survive you being in the sea and having to be rescued by a dolphin."

"Mum and Dad will get you another one." Lillie sighed. "But I won't have any pocket money for years. They'll make me pay it back."

"Upgrade!" Frankie said, laughing. She stroked Lillie's hair, trying to separate out the clinging wet tangles. "Lillie, what were you doing? I thought maybe you came down to the beach to look for the dolphins again, as you seemed to love them so much. I wanted to find you and bring you back before Mum and Dad noticed you were gone. Did you walk into the water again? You were so far out! What were you thinking?"

"I wasn't on the beach." Lillie looked sideways at her sister. "I walked across the causeway to Worm's Head. I wanted to climb up to the high bit – and I did! I went further than all of us! So that you and Lara couldn't say I was a baby. I've got photos, loads of them. I saw the seals again, and the blowhole by Devil's Bridge." She sighed. "I did have them."

"The photos might have uploaded before the phone died," Frankie told her. "You never know."

"Yeah, maybe."

"I don't think you're a baby," Frankie said, after a little silence.

Lillie didn't answer her. She wasn't going to tell her sister that everything was OK, just like that. Frankie didn't get forgiven all that easily, even if Lillie had lost her phone.

"You haven't said how you ended up in the sea," Frankie went on slowly. "What happened?"

Lillie sighed. "I was on the island, and I–I kind of forgot the time. I was upset with you! And it made me really tired. I was half asleep and I stopped thinking about getting back before the tide came in. Then I remembered and I thought I could still make it. I tried to go back over the causeway too late."

Frankie pulled away to look at Lillie properly, her eyes wide and horrified. "You knew that was dangerous – Mum kept on telling us about the tide!"

Lillie scowled down at her wet trainers. "Yes, but I didn't want to call for help. Everyone would have laughed at me. You already called me babyish, it would have been even worse if I had to get rescued!"

Frankie's mouth twisted. "So you went off on your own because of me, and then you didn't get help because of me," she said quietly.

"It was Lara too," Lillie muttered. "And you did come to find me."

"Yeah, after it was me that got you into trouble in the first place…" She shook her head. "Lara wouldn't come with me and help look for you, you know? She said you'd just gone off in a sulk and she didn't care.

Not even when I said I was sure there was something wrong. I begged her and she just laughed at me. I can't believe I spent all that time hanging out with her this holiday. Letting her boss me about." Frankie hesitated. "It made me feel good, that was all. She's so cool. At least I thought she was. She's older, and she always looks beautiful, and she's done so much stuff…"

"Just because she's done cool things doesn't mean she has to go on about it all the time," Lillie pointed out.

Frankie snorted a laugh. "Yeah, that's true. She doesn't shut up, does she?" She sighed. "I think Mum and Dad will have noticed that you're gone by now, Lillie. We should go back." She hugged Lillie a little harder. "What do you want to tell them? We can

just say you went for a walk and got lost,
if you like."

"And got soaking wet and destroyed
your phone?"

"Mmmm. Maybe not." She looked Lillie up and down anxiously. "You look so cold. Maybe you ought to go to A&E, just to make sure you're OK…" She sighed. "Actually, I wouldn't put it past Lara to be making a big fuss about you being missing now. For the drama, you know. I'll tell Mum and Dad it was my fault."

"But it was her as well…" Lillie grumbled.

"I know. But she's never going to admit to anything, is she?" Frankie got to her feet, pulling Lillie up after her. "Mind you, I think Gran noticed the way we were being. I kept spotting her watching us. I don't think Lara's going to get everything her own way." She led Lillie over the sand, stumbling in her heavy, sea-soaked trainers, and they started the long climb up the steps to head back to the village.

Lillie stopped to catch her breath about

halfway up and turned to look back at the sea. Worm's Head was completely cut off now, there was no sign that anyone could ever walk out to the island.

And against the green sea-dragon cliffs, she could see four small grey shapes, arcing gracefully in and out of the water as they headed out to sea. Lillie watched them for a few seconds, just by herself. It felt as though the dolphins were there only for her, and she loved them.

She could have turned away and walked on, and she did think about it for just a moment. But then she pulled gently at her sister's sleeve.

"Frankie, look, I can see the dolphins!"

Frankie put up her hand to shield her eyes, gazing out over the glittering blue water.

"Where? Oh! I see them too!"

Without really planning it, both of them lifted a hand to wave, and then they climbed on up the steps, together.

THE LOST BEAR CUB

From MULTI-MILLION best-selling author

Holly Webb

Illustrated by David Dean

1

"Lucy...Wake up, sweetheart. We're nearly there. Hey... Lucy..."

Lucy blinked and snuggled further into the fleecy blanket Mum had wrapped around her. She'd spent ages trying to get to sleep on the plane but it had all been too different and strange. She'd even enjoyed the aeroplane food. It might not have tasted very nice but it had been fun, opening all the little boxes and packets.

"I've only been asleep a minute," she murmured, blinking around at the bright cabin. There was an energy in the air now – people were folding their blankets away and searching through the seat pockets. A garbled announcement came over the speaker.

"We'll be landing soon," her mum explained. "You need to put your seat belt on. Can you feel the plane going down?"

Lucy frowned as she fiddled with the fastening of her seat belt, wondering how she would know. She'd never been on a plane before – but actually, her ears felt strange. Was that it? "I think my ears are popping."

"I've got some mints you can suck, that'll help."

Dad leaned over, smiling at her. He looked so excited, Lucy thought. He'd been like that for months. Ever since they'd started to plan their trip to Canada. Dad's only brother, Lucy's uncle Pete, had gone to live in Canada years before. Lucy had never met him, and though they all said hello to each other on video calls – Lucy and her big brother Jack and their uncle's children too – it wasn't the same as really knowing someone.

Now they were going to stay for a whole month of the summer holidays at Uncle Pete and Auntie Cass's house. There were two older boy cousins, Reuben and Sam, and Kitty who was about six months older than Lucy. Lucy was as excited as Dad but she was nervous too. What if they didn't get on with their cousins? Just because they were family didn't mean they were actually going to *like* each other. Lucy loved spending time with her friends at school but she didn't think she was very good at meeting new people. She never knew what to say. Mum, Dad and Lucy's friends from school who'd known her for ages said she was really funny but someone she'd just met wouldn't know it.

Lucy had two other cousins back in England, Georgie and Marcus, but they were younger than she was. They loved her and Jack because they were big and grown up. Now Lucy was going to be the youngest and the quietest… What if she spent the summer holidays hardly talking at all?

Lucy unwrapped the mint her dad had given her and slipped it into her mouth. She wasn't going to worry about all that now. Dad had kept saying it was going to be an adventure – they were going to camp out, and there would be all this amazing wildlife to see. Uncle Pete had sent them photos of moose walking down

the street near where he lived, and even a bear
sunbathing in a neighbour's garden.

"Look!" Jack nudged her and pointed out of
the window, and Lucy leaned over to see past
her brother.

"Wow," she whispered,
peering down
through the clouds.
"Mountains! They
look so big. Is that
snow on the top?"
It had been really
sunny and hot
back at home, so
it felt odd to see
patches of snow
snaking down the
rocky crags.

"They're very tall, so they probably have a bit of snow all year round," Dad said, craning over from his seat on the other side of the aisle. "Not long now!"

Lucy threaded her hand with Mum's as they both stared out of the window. Her ears felt very odd, as though someone was pressing their hands around the sides of her head, but the view outside was so amazing that she could almost ignore it.

"Look at that lake!" Jack pointed again. Lucy leaned as far as she could and spotted the jewel-bright blue water against the dark mountains.

"It's beautiful," she murmured. It all looked so different too, wild and strange and magical. Lucy's nervousness was still there a little but the excitement was taking over. There was a city of skyscrapers below them now, with the mountains rising up behind and the sea stretching round. Lucy had never seen anything like it before – she couldn't wait to land.

An hour later, all the sleep Lucy hadn't had on the plane was catching up with her. She tried to swallow a yawn and the airport official checking their passports smiled. "You can't be tired now. I bet you've got a full day ahead of you."

Lucy nodded shyly, loving the Canadian accent.

"You're all done. Welcome to Vancouver!"

"Thank you!" Mum put her arm round Lucy and scooted them forwards. "We need to head for baggage reclaim and get our suitcases," she explained to Jack and Lucy.

"And I can send a message to Pete, telling

him we're nearly ready for him to pick us up,"
Dad said. "Their house is about a forty-five-
minute drive away." He looked round at the
bustling airport and shook his head. "Hard to
believe, isn't it? There's the busy city and then
the wild mountains, and they're practically next
to each other!"

It took longer than Lucy could have believed
to get their luggage – they seemed to be
watching the same suitcases that weren't theirs
go round the carousel for ages – but at last they
appeared and they grabbed them then headed
through the airport to meet Uncle Pete.

Lucy hadn't realized how much he'd look like
Dad when they saw him for real, standing by
the barrier and waving. In photos and on video
calls he and Dad didn't seem alike at all but
it was something about the way they stood.

It made her like Uncle Pete at once.

"I wish I could have brought everybody," he said, taking one of the big suitcases after he'd given them a hug. "The whole family wanted to come to greet you. But we wouldn't have all been able to fit in the car. I've sorted out hiring one for you while you're here."

Lucy trotted along after them, wheeling her bag and trying not to bump into people. She stifled another yawn, wishing she'd slept more on the plane. She didn't want to miss any of their first view of Canada.

Mum sat in the middle of the back seat so Lucy and Jack could be by the windows. The airport was on an island but once they'd got over the bridges to the mainland, the first part of the journey looked a lot like their drive to the airport back home. Lots of shops and houses – and cars.

Until they came out of the edges of the city and started to see flashes of startlingly blue water between the dark pine trees, and mountains on the other side of the water. It all looked wild and exciting, even from inside a car.

"Those are more islands over there," Uncle Pete called from the front seat. "You're seeing it on a good day. It's beautiful with the sun on the water."

"Oh…" Lucy whispered, as a break in the trees showed them the ruffled surface of the water, its ripples glinting in the sun.

Uncle Pete laughed. "That's how I felt when I first saw it, Lucy. It's the most beautiful place to live. Here." He rustled about in the pocket of the car door and passed back a handful of leaflets. "Here, you two, take a look at these – some of the amazing places we're going to take you to."

Lucy and Jack flicked through them, looking at hiking trails, a kayaking centre and camping grounds. "Mum, look…" Lucy whispered, holding up a leaflet about a campsite. Across the top, in big black capitals, it said:

THIS IS
BEAR COUNTRY

"Same here," Jack said, pointing at another one.

"What's that?" Dad said, turning round in his seat. "Wow, bears, they don't want you to miss that, do they?"

Uncle Pete snorted. "No, they do not. We have to be so careful round here. Often people get themselves into trouble because they don't take it seriously; they think the bears are cute. Mind you, I think moose are more dangerous than bears." He slowed the car, shaking his head. "Uh-oh, I shouldn't have said anything. Hey, you two, look out the front."

"Is that a moose?" Jack yelped.

"Two. A mother and a calf." Uncle Pete sounded quite proud, as though he'd laid on the moose specially. "You see them quite often along here. We have to watch out when we're driving. Mostly it's deer on the roads but you get moose too, and sometimes a bear..."

The moose were just strolling across the road, as though they hadn't a care in the world. They didn't seem bothered about the cars – perhaps they knew that everyone would stop for them. The mother was huge, definitely taller than Dad, Lucy thought.

She had a long, blunt nose, a bit like a camel, and such spindly legs. Her baby padded behind her, looking tiny next to its huge mother.

"Such big ears," Mum said, watching as the two moose disappeared into the trees. "But no horns?"

"Only the bull moose have those," Uncle Pete explained. "They're usually a lot bigger as well."

"Even bigger than that…" Lucy murmured. "How old was that baby one, Uncle Pete?"

"I think they're usually born at the beginning of summer," her uncle said thoughtfully. "Around June? So maybe a couple of months old. Definitely a lucky spot on your first day. We'll have to see what else we can find to top that!"

"They're here!"

Lucy could hear someone shouting excitedly even before Uncle Pete stopped the car and then what seemed like a huge number of people spilled out of the house to meet them. Dad opened Lucy's door and she climbed out slowly, looking at her cousins. Luckily Reuben was a lot taller than Sam so it was easy to tell them apart. She was just noticing that he had darker

hair too, when someone suddenly hugged her and she squeaked. Her cousin Kitty had run round the side of the car without Lucy realizing.

"Hey, Lucy! I'm Kitty, your cousin. Did you have a good journey? Did you like the plane? Were you airsick? I get sick whenever I'm in a plane. And cars sometimes."

"Hi…" Lucy gazed at her, a bit daunted by the flood of words – but at least her cousin seemed friendly. Kitty was smaller than she was, Lucy realized, feeling a bit pleased. She was the youngest child there but at least she wasn't the smallest.

"Wow, you're really tall." Kitty stepped back and eyed her, looking a bit surprised. "I thought I'd be taller than you since I'm older. I'm ten."

"I'm ten in September," Lucy told her. It wasn't that long.

"You're staying in my room – I've got a bed that pulls out from underneath mine. Want me to help carry your stuff?"

"Um, thanks." Lucy handed Kitty her little backpack and walked round to the back of the car to grab her suitcase. Her cousin seemed really friendly, which was good. And it would be fun sharing a room – she'd never done that before, except on a few sleepovers with friends from school.

"Everyone got all their stuff?" Uncle Pete asked, peering into the back of the car. "No one left any snacks or anything in the seat pockets?" He grinned at Kitty as he said it but it sounded like he was serious. Lucy shook her head uncertainly. Was he worried about things getting left in the car and going off? Mum had got really annoyed with Jack once for leaving an apple core in the car door where it started to grow horrible grey furry mildew.

"I don't think Jack or Lucy had any snacks…"

Mum said – she sounded uncertain too.

"It's not that I'm fussy about the car," Uncle Pete explained. "You know I said we have to be careful about bears. I really meant it. If you leave food in the car they can break in looking for it. It's not a problem if it's in the trunk and well covered up, but wrappers and stuff in the back, that's just asking for trouble."

Jack and Kitty exchanged a glance. Was Uncle Pete having them on?

"Hang on, how would bears know about the food?" Dad asked, looking puzzled.

"They've got the most amazing sense of smell," Uncle Pete said. "And believe it or not, they can open car doors, even if they're locked. Car doors don't stand up to five centimetres of claws, not when a bear wants in. It's absolutely true, Martin, I promise. It actually happened to me not long after I moved out here. I parked up the car close to a trail and went hiking, and I'd left some supplies on the back seat. I locked the car, but it was an old model and the bear didn't have much trouble getting in. It ate all the food and ripped the seats to shreds in case I was hiding anything else." Uncle Pete shrugged. "Now I always check. A bear might have more of a problem with a newer car, but it's not worth the risk."

"Dad! You never told us that!" Reuben shook his head, laughing.

"It's not just food either," Auntie Cass put in. "Anything with a strong, sweet sort of smell, like a packet of wet wipes."

Mum looked worriedly at their bags, and Lucy knew she was thinking that she usually had wet wipes in her handbag, just in case.

"I don't think you got them out in the car," she whispered, and Mum smiled.

"I think we've got a lot to learn while we're here," she whispered back. "You definitely didn't have any biscuits or anything from the flight that you left in there? It would be awful if a bear ruined Uncle Pete's car…"

Lucy shuddered. Mum was right – that would *not* be a good start to the holiday.

Illustrated by Dawn Cooper

THE WILDMEADOW HARE

From MULTI-MILLION best-selling author

Holly Webb

Ellie used to love watching the hares leap
and play on the common with her mum.
But since Mum passed away it's getting
harder to remember those happy memories.

Until one day, Ellie finds an injured baby
hare. The poor animal looks so scared,
she has to do something to help. Nursing
the hare back to health will be a big
responsibility, but could it be Ellie's chance
to feel close to her mum again?

THE DAWN SEAL

From MULTI-MILLION best-selling author

Holly Webb

Illustrated by David Dean

Lissa was so excited to spend the summer on her dad's houseboat. She thought they'd have lots of exciting adventures, but her dad's job means that he's too busy to spend much time with her. Lissa can't help but feel lonely and starts to miss her mum and sister back home.

Then one morning, she spots a lost seal pup in the river. She starts waking up at dawn every day to catch a glimpse of this beautiful creature. Lissa wants to help her find her way home, but can she protect the young seal without scaring her away?

HOLLY WEBB

Holly Webb started out as a children's book editor and wrote her first series for the publisher she worked for. She has been writing ever since, with over one hundred and fifty books to her name. Holly lives in Berkshire, with her husband and three children. Holly's pet cats are always nosying around when she is trying to type on her laptop.

For more information
about Holly Webb visit:

www.holly-webb.com